Garfield's PET FORCE™

K-NINER & DOG OF DOOM!

Other titles in this series:

Garfield's Pet Force #1:
The Outrageous Origin

Garfield's Pet Force #2:
Pie-Rat's Revenge!

Produced by Creative Media Applications, Inc., and Paws Incorporated

Graphics by Jeff Wesley

ISBN 0-590-05944-0

12 11 10 9 8 7 6 5 4 3 2   8 9/9 0 1 2 3/0

Printed in the U.S.A.   40

First Scholastic printing, May 1998

Garfield's PET FORCE™

K-NINER & DOG OF DOOM!

Created by
Jim Davis

Character development by
Mark Acey & Gary Barker

Written by
Michael Teitelbaum

Illustrated by
Gary Barker & Larry Fentz

SCHOLASTIC INC.
New York Toronto London Auckland Sydney

Introduction

When a group of lovable pets — Garfield, Odie, Arlene, Nermal, and Pooky — are transported to an alternate universe, they become a mighty superhero team known as . . . *Pet Force*!

Garzooka — Large and in charge, he is the fearless and famished leader of Pet Force. He's a ferocious feline with nerves of steel, a razor-sharp right claw, and the awesome ability to fire gamma-radiated hairballs (as well as deadly one-liners) from his mouth.

Odious — Although utterly clueless, he possesses incredible strength, ultra-slippery slobber, and a super-stretchy stun tongue. One zap of his lethal wet tongue causes a total mental meltdown in anyone he unleashes it upon.

Starlena — Sings a *purrfectly* pitched siren song ("the meow that wows!"). Anyone who hears her hypnotic song immediately falls into a trance — except Garzooka.

Abnermal — Has a body temperature of absolute zero; one touch of his icy paw freezes foes in their tracks. He can extend a nuke-proof force field to protect himself, as well as the other Pet Force members. His pester-power — more annoying than your little brother! — is one power that Garzooka could live without.

Compooky — Part-computer/part-teddy, this cyberbear extraordinaire is not only incredibly cute, but is also the mental giant of the team (not that big a deal).

Behold the mighty Pet Force! *Let the fur fly!*

1

The story so far . . .

There are many universes parallel to our own. Each of these universes is very much like ours, but each one differs in some ways. For example, in our universe Jon Arbuckle is a nice but dim-witted pet owner. But in another universe, the particular parallel universe that concerns our story, Jon is a nice but dim-witted *emperor*. In our universe, Garfield, Odie, Nermal, and Arlene are pets, and Pooky is a teddy bear. In the parallel universe ruled by Emperor Jon, these five friends are the superpowered heroes known as Pet Force.

In Emperor Jon's universe, the evil veterinarian Vetvix has vowed to conquer the universe and replace Jon as its ruler. But first, Vetvix must defeat Pet Force. To reach her goal, Vetvix has created an army of mutant animals to serve her, each transformed, through her experiments, to be extra-powerful and extra-evil.

Vetvix had sent one of these mutant animals, Space Pie-Rat, to defeat Pet Force. He failed, and as punishment, Vetvix cast a spell that turned him into a mouse. Pie-Rat was captured by Pet Force and taken to a cage in Emperor Jon's palace where he became the emperor's pet. He managed to escape and fell into a cauldron of magic brew prepared by the emperor's sorcerer, Binky. The brew turned Pie-Rat back into a giant rat. Then he grew to *twice* his normal size, a whopping twelve feet in height.

Stealing Pet Force's spaceship, the *Lightspeed Lasagna*, Pie-Rat returned to take his revenge on Vetvix. Using a vial of Sorceror Binky's magic brew, Pie-Rat reduced Vetvix to a tiny, doll-sized version of herself. He then stole her magic power crystal. When he placed the crystal on a necklace around his neck, it gave him incredibly evil power.

The five heroes of Pet Force chased Pie-Rat in their homemade spaceship, the *Planetary Pizza*. They tracked Pie-Rat to Vetvix's hideout where, during a titanic battle, Garzooka took the necklace from Pie-Rat and put it on himself. The dark magic of the power crystal instantly turned Garzooka evil, and he and Pie-Rat set off on a spree of looting and feasting across the galaxy.

The other members of Pet Force caught up to the evil Garzooka and Pie-Rat. Starlena cut the crystal from Garzooka's necklace. In the process, the magic crystal shattered into pieces, Garzooka was freed from its evil spell, and Pie-Rat was captured.

Later, Sorcerer Binky's magic brew wore off Pie-Rat and Vetvix, and they both were restored to their original sizes. Pie-Rat escaped with the shattered pieces of the power crystal in the *Planetary Pizza*. Vetvix, meanwhile, set up a new hideout where she began her latest experiment, another plan to seize control of Emperor Jon's universe!

2

The parallel universe . . .

Deep in the far reaches of Emperor Jon's universe, a floating fortress orbited high above a planet. This planet was many light-years from the emperor's home planet, Polyester. In a hidden laboratory within the fortress, the evil Vetvix was putting the finishing touches on her latest experiment.

After the location of her last hideout had been discovered by her former ally and now enemy Space Pie-Rat, Vetvix decided to set up her new base of operations as far from Polyester as she could. She thought her *Floating Fortress of Fear* was far enough away to be safely hidden from her enemies.

In her lab, Vetvix stood before a control panel, making the final adjustments for her experiment. Thick cables ran from the control panel across the lab to a tall rectangular energization booth. Vetvix increased the power to the booth, which hummed and glowed with a sickly green evil energy.

"At last, my most powerful creation is almost complete," she said. Her face grew intense as the hum coming from the booth reached an almost deafening pitch. Then suddenly, the lab was silent. "It is done!" Vetvix yelled.

Inside the energization booth stood the result of her latest sinister plan. His name was K-Niner. Once just an ordinary Doberman pinscher, K-Niner now stood upright like a human, nearly six feet tall. His already powerful body had grown in strength from the energy that had bombarded him in the booth. Huge muscles rippled along his mighty arms and across his broad chest. Vetvix had handpicked him from a litter because he had a nasty, ruthless personality. She knew he would make a powerful warrior.

K-Niner had just received his final dose of brain-boosting radiation. This treatment increased his intelligence to match his new, super-powerful body. With the treatment finished, K-Niner stepped from the energization booth glowing with power. His muscles bulged, his strong jaw had grown to twice its normal size, and his sleek black coat reflected the bright lights of the lab. Then he spoke.

"I say, old girl," began K-Niner. "Your clever device is quite a success. I believe this surge of new intelligence I'm feeling is quite amazing indeed!

Not to mention my increased strength and chiseled biceps!"

Vetvix was stunned. Along with K-Niner's boosted intelligence and giant muscles, she had programmed him with the power of human speech. However, K-Niner, for some unknown reason, had acquired a British accent. Vetvix had wanted to create a terrible, vicious creature, but K-Niner sounded more like he would offer you a nice cup of tea than rip your throat out with his teeth.

"What have I done?" shrieked Vetvix. "I wanted to create a savage killer who could defeat Pet Force. It sounds like I ended up with a polite butler!"

K-Niner's beady, jet-black eyes narrowed. He grabbed Vetvix by the throat and lifted her off her feet. "No, no, no, my dear," he said with as much of a snarl as he could muster. "Don't let my fancy way of speaking fool you. I'll rip your throat out in a nanosecond and have it for lunch. Understand?"

Vetvix was relieved that her creation only *appeared* gentle. She was, however, annoyed that he would have the nerve to grab her by the throat. *I'm pleased*, she thought, *but he needs to learn his place. He needs to learn that I am his master.*

With K-Niner still clutching her neck, Vetvix muttered a magical spell in a half-choked voice. K-Niner immediately loosened his grasp, then collapsed in a heap at Vetvix's feet.

7

"I'm so glad to see that you're as ferocious as I had hoped," said Vetvix. "But if you ever lay a paw on me again, I'll remove your brain with a fork and feed it to Gorbull! Understand?"

Gorbull was Vetvix's beloved pet, the result of her first experiment in combining animals. The mutant half-gorilla/half-pit bull lifted his head and licked his lips at the thought of chowing down on K-Niner's brain.

"Point well-taken, I must admit," replied K-Niner, getting to his feet and brushing himself off. "Now, how may I be of service, your evilness?"

Vetvix smiled. "Use your newly boosted brain-power and think about this," she told him. "How do you feel about the fact that humans treat dogs with such disrespect? You know, forcing them to sit on command, fetch sticks, wear leashes, the whole pet thing."

K-Niner thought for a second, then replied. "Absolutely uncivilized," he said. "I think it's high time that dogs — a most noble species — stop playing second violin to humans."

"My feelings precisely," said Vetvix. "I created you to lead a dog liberation movement. I want you to free all the dogs so they can take over this universe. Let people see how it feels to wear the leash and roll over for *your* amusement."

"Sounds simply brilliant!" exclaimed K-Niner. "But what do *you* get out of it?"

"The animals will control the humans, and *I* will

control the animals," replied Vetvix. "I will use this opportunity to enslave the humans, including Emperor Jon. Then his universe will be mine!"

"Bravo!" cheered K-Niner. "I see you've thought this through. Now, by what means do I carry out your plan?"

"Look at this, my fierce friend," answered Vetvix. Opening a locked storage bin, she pulled out a huge weapon. The weapon, developed by Vetvix in her lab, looked like a giant, hand-held bazooka with lots of gadgets. Instead of firing bullets or laser beams, this weapon sent out waves of brain-boosting radiation.

"This device is a portable brain-boosting weapon," explained Vetvix. "It is set to work only on the brains of dogs, so you can fire this weapon at an entire city and only the dogs in that city will be affected. Their minds will be boosted in a way similar to yours. Once the dogs' intelligence is boosted, taking control and enslaving their human masters should be easy, since dogs possess superior fighting and survival abilities.

"I will also supply you with these electronic enslavement collars." Vetvix pulled out a steel collar that buzzed with a low electric hum. "Using your superior abilities, you will place these collars around the necks of the humans. Then they will be powerless to resist the commands of their new masters — the dogs!"

K-Niner smiled and flexed his newly enlarged muscles. "I am humbled and in your service, madam," he said in his soft, proper voice.

"Now take one of my spaceships and an army of my mutant warriors, you Despicable Doberman of Doom, and set in motion the beginning of the end of human domination. A new day will soon dawn when the enslaved humans of the universe will bow down to *Emperor Vetvix!*"

K-Niner left for his mission with an army of mutant animals and a spaceship full of brain-boosting weapons and electronic enslavement collars. Vetvix now turned to a bit of unfinished personal business. She settled into a comfortable position on a cushion in her sleep chamber. Vetvix then closed her eyes and began to meditate. She reached out with her psychic powers, searching for the energy given off by her power crystal. She was cosmically connected to this energy.

Vetvix's evil mind drifted through the universe. She knew that the crystal would lead her to Pie-Rat, who had stolen it from her. Once she located the missing gem she would retrieve it and destroy Pie-Rat in one swift move.

Slowly Vetvix's mind probed the far corners of the universe until she finally recognized the energy pattern that could be given off only by her crystal.

"Shattered!" she shrieked, breaking out of her trance. "That fool has shattered my precious crystal." Then she laughed softly. "Knowing Pie-Rat as I do, I'll bet that he's going to try to find someone to restore the damaged crystal," she murmured to herself, smiling. "I know exactly where his search will lead him. And when he arrives, I'll be waiting!"

3

Our universe, Jon's living room . . .

It was a bright spring afternoon. Jon Arbuckle stood in his living room dressed in red-and-white plaid shorts, a sunshine-yellow Hawaiian shirt, and bright orange sneakers. He had covered himself with half a bottle of sunblock and his skin now gleamed with a greasy sheen. He looked like a turkey that had been basting in the oven for several hours — that is, a turkey wearing plaid shorts, a Hawaiian shirt, and sneakers. Jon held a volleyball under his arm. Every few seconds the ball squirted away, sliding against the slippery sunscreen that coated the inside of his arm.

"Okay!" shouted Jon, picking the ball up off the floor for the tenth time. "The net's all set up. Who's ready to go outside for a game of volleyball?"

Jon's pets were sprawled out around the living room. Garfield had his head under the couch, trying to pretend no one else was around while he snuck in a nap. Pooky sat cuddled faithfully at his side. Odie was staring intently at a corner of the room. He hadn't stared at this particular corner for a few days and he was just checking to make sure that nothing had changed since he last looked there. Arlene was lazily thumbing through a magazine, and Nermal was reorganizing his comic book collection for the fourth time that week. No one budged at Jon's offer of a volleyball game.

"Come on, guys," whined Jon. "It's been raining all week. We've been stuck in the house for days. Who wants to be stuck inside on a gorgeous afternoon like today?"

All four pets raised their hands at once. Garfield raised Pooky's paw.

"You guys are unbelievable!" Jon pleaded. "I can't play volleyball all by myself! What am I going to do?"

Start walking away from the house and keep walking until you've counted to a million, thought Garfield. *Then continue walking and try for two million.*

"I'll make a huge pan of lasagna for you after the volleyball game," promised Jon, knowing that if he could get Garfield to move the others might follow.

Garfield pulled his head out from under the couch, thinking about a steaming pan of fresh lasagna. He started to drool. *It sounds great,* he thought, *but if I have to do some exercise first, what's the point?*

Jon's high, whining voice continued to fill the room, grating on the nerves of his pets. Torn between the lasagna and the chance to sleep, Garfield slowly got to his feet — he couldn't sleep while Jon was complaining. "Well, as long as I'm standing here, I might as well go out to the backyard," he grumbled to himself. Jon grinned as he saw Garfield head toward the back door.

The parallel universe. The planet Kennel...

The planet Kennel was known throughout the universe as a place where dogs were well loved. Most of the population kept dogs as pets. In fact, there were more dogs on Kennel than on any other planet in Emperor Jon's universe. That is precisely why K-Niner chose this planet to begin his reign of terror.

The huge battle cruiser that Vetvix had given to K-Niner was filled with her mutant animal creations. These creatures served as loyal soldiers in Vetvix's army, with K-Niner as the commanding officer.

"I say, you there," K-Niner called out, pointing to a half-frog/half-rabbit. "Hop on over to the kitchen and bring me a cup of hot tea and a plate of buttered scones."

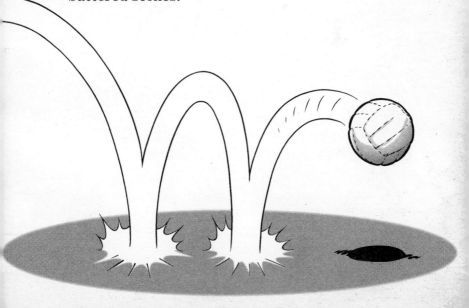

The creature wig-
gled its pink nose,
then hopped away
on its powerful,
green hind legs. A
short while later, it returned
carrying a tray that held a cup of hot melted
butter and a soggy scone floating in a dish of
lukewarm tea.

K-Niner sighed and shook his head. Then he
slapped the tray out of the frightened creature's
hands. The tray and its contents crashed to the
ground as the frog-rabbit scurried away.

"No problem, boss. I've got you covered," said a
gravelly voice from beside K-Niner.

The Despicable Doberman of Doom looked over
and saw a giant crow with a turtle's head. "You
want your little snack, you've got it, boss!" said
the bizarre-looking creature.

"I am quite stunned that you actually have the
power of speech," said K-Niner.

"Oh, yeah, sure," replied the turtle-crow.
"Vetvix tested her brain-boosting ray on a few of
us to work out the kinks before she made you," he
explained. "I was one of her early test cases.
Wilbur's the name. Now sit tight, boss. I'll be right
back!"

A few moments later, Wilbur returned. "Here
you go, boss," he said, handing a plate and a cup to

K-Niner. "A hot T-shirt and some scattered bones. Just what you ordered."

"I can see why Vetvix continued to work out the kinks in her brain-boosting ray before she used it on me," said K-Niner. "Never mind. I'll just get the tea myself. I only hope all of you are better at fighting than you are at catering!" K-Niner prepared himself a snack as the battle cruiser continued on its journey.

The massive spaceship reached the planet Kennel a few days later. Once they had landed, K-Niner led his army to a small village on a remote corner of the planet.

"I do believe that this is a most important occasion," K-Niner announced to his army. His proper British accent masked his viciousness. "The dog liberation movement begins here. We will start in this tiny village, freeing the enslaved

dogs one by one. When we have switched the balance of power in this town and the dogs rule, we will move on, town by town, city by city, until all the dogs on the planet of Kennel are liberated."

K-Niner pulled out Vetvix's brain-boosting ray

and fired the huge weapon at the dogs in the village. As the brain-boosting radiation struck, dogs began to rise onto their back legs, startled to discover that their intelligence had increased. They were now able to speak and think.

K-Niner spoke into a bullhorn, trying to get the dog population excited and angry. "Fellow canines, so good of you to join me in the joys of increased intelligence," he called. "Aren't you tired of living to serve your human masters? They don't

really love you, as they claim. They don't respect you. They just like having power over you."

Cries of "Yeah!" "You're not kidding!" and "Who is this guy? He's pretty smart!" came from the crowd of dogs that quickly assembled in front of K-Niner.

He continued. "Are you fed up with begging for food? Tired of performing tricks for treats?"

The mob of dogs grew larger and more riled up by the second. Angry screams and growls filled the air as K-Niner brought his carefully rehearsed speech to a fevered pitch.

"You've now got the intelligence to turn the tables, old chaps," K-Niner explained. "My soldiers are, at this very moment, walking among you and handing out electronic enslavement collars for you to place on your former masters. These powerful collars will make *you* the masters from now on. Use your superior strength and newly boosted intelligence to take control of your planet and your lives. Your canine brothers and sisters all over Kennel will soon do the same. In a short while *we* will be the ones giving the humans tick baths."

"Yeah, let's see how *they* like those stupid tick baths!" came a cry from the crowd. "I hate those baths!"

"So let a new day dawn!" continued K-Niner, the crowd of dogs now fully on his side. "A day of total dog freedom and human enslavement!"

As K-Niner whipped the crowd into a frenzy, his army of mutant animals spread throughout the mob and handed out the electronic enslavement collars. When the Despicable Doberman of Doom finished his speech, the brain-boosted dogs went back to their homes with evil in their hearts.

A dog named Tippy, a mixed breed who was normally very gentle, burst into his master's house.

"Tippy's home!" the master called to his wife. "And he's walking on his hind legs! That's a new trick, Tippy. Good boy. Would you like a doggie treat for learning your new trick?"

"What I'd like is for you to stop talking to me like I'm a brainless fool," said Tippy.

Tippy's master turned pale. "Honey, the dog is talking!" he shouted.

"Stop fooling around and just give him a doggie treat for learning his new trick," came the reply from the next room.

"The other thing I'd like is for you to put this on!" growled Tippy, holding out the electronic collar he had received from K-Niner. *"Now!"*

The enraged dog knocked his master to the ground and forced the collar around his neck. When the man tried to get to his feet, Tippy turned up the power on the collar's controller leash. The human collapsed in a heap on the floor, his face a twisted mask of pain.

"Now *I* am the master, and it's *your* turn to roll over!" snarled Tippy. The man rolled around on the living room floor, crashing into couches and tables.

"Honey," came the voice from the next room. "Don't wrestle with the dog. You know it gets him overly excited."

Tippy took another collar and headed for the next room.

In homes throughout the village, dogs confronted their owners until finally all the humans had been subdued. Soon dogs were running the village. The humans were given tick baths. They were forced to beg for food from their new canine masters. They were made to do tricks like rolling over, sitting, shaking hands, fetching sticks, and begging.

At the edge of town, K-Niner addressed his troops. "On to the next village, gents," he ordered. "I must say, this brain-boosting is positively smashing. Why, in no time at all, we'll have this entire planet under our control. Then our dog liberation movement will spread — all the way to Emperor Jon's home planet, Polyester!" He snickered an evil — but polite — snicker and led his troops to the next village.

4

Emperor Jon sat at his royal desk in the throne room of his palace on the planet Polyester. The gold crown on his head was tipped slightly to one side. His long robes flowed down to the floor. His desk was actually a plastic folding card table. Emperor Jon preferred it to the ornate, hand-carved, antique oak desk that had been in the throne room when he became emperor.

Jon was sorting through computer printouts of tax lists and business plans, attending to the usual day-to-day details that went along with being the ultimate authority of the universe. The emperor had been at it all morning. The words and numbers on the pages in front of him all began to blur together.

"Now let's see," the emperor muttered to himself, punching numbers into a calculator. "Here's a request for some aid from the planet Aqua, where there's been an awful lot of flooding lately. Hmm.

I'll send them a huge sponge. That should do the trick.

"Now what have we here? There's a metal shortage on the planet Plastic. I've got two extra boxes of paper clips here. I'll send them right along. That should start to enrich their iron-poor planet." Emperor Jon giggled at his own joke, knowing there was little chance anyone else would, even if there had been someone else in the room. Then he picked up the daily economic reports.

"Grain prices are going down, grain elevators are going up, and I'm getting a mi*graine* headache just thinking about all this stuff," he moaned, putting down the papers. "Oh, dear. Maybe my advisors are right. Maybe I should hire a royal accountant to handle all of this number crunching.

"Which reminds me," said Emperor Jon, putting down his pencil and getting up from the plastic folding chair that matched the desk, "I've got some number crunching to attend to over here." Jon walked over to his throne — a vinyl-upholstered reclining chair — and picked up the bag of chips he had left there the night before. "That's one," he counted, popping a chip into his mouth and crunching away. "Two," he added, crunching another chip.

Within a few seconds, Jon had completely lost interest in the business of running the universe and was making a private bet with himself as to how many chips he would find in the bag. "I guess fifty-two," he said. "But there's really only one way to find out for sure!" Jon went back to eating, crunching, and counting his chips.

Suddenly an explosion outside shook the palace. Jon raced to his window and looked out. He saw a tiny spaceship that had crashed right on the front lawn. The ship was on fire, and palace guards and medical teams rushed to see if there was anyone inside.

"I've got to get down there!" shouted Jon. "I'll finish number crunching later." He put down his bag of chips and raced from the throne room.

By the time Emperor Jon reached the front lawn, the emergency crews had pulled a man from the little ship, which was in flames. "Is this man all right?" demanded the emperor.

"He doesn't seem to be hurt physically, your highness," reported the palace doctor, "but he keeps saying and doing the strangest things."

The man immediately rolled over on the ground, then got onto his knees, lifted his hands up near his chin, and said, "Ruff! Ruff! Grrrrr. Roll over, sit up, beg. Good doggie, good doggie." Then he rolled onto his back and waved his belly at the emperor.

"I think he wants you to scratch his belly, your highness," said a palace guard.

"Well, of course he does," said the emperor, who knelt down and began to scratch the man's belly.

"Wait a minute!" shouted Jon, realizing what he was doing. "This is not a dog. It's a man." Then Jon noticed a tight-fitting collar around the man's neck. It glowed with eerie green light. The man clutched at the collar, trying to pull it off, but it wouldn't budge. He then reached up with his foot and scratched at the collar.

"Guards, remove that collar at once," ordered the emperor. "It seems to be hurting him."

Using a carefully aimed beam from his laser weapon, a palace guard split the collar in half. It fell to the floor and the glowing stopped. The man shook his head and slowly rose to his feet.

"Thank you, your highness. You've saved me," said the man in a choked, raspy voice.

"What is going on here?" asked the emperor — a question he asked at least four times a day.

"I am from the planet Kennel," the man explained. "Two days ago a creature called K-Niner landed on my planet in a huge battle cruiser. This K-Niner is a dog, but not just a dog."

"He's also a cat?" asked Jon.

"No, your highness," replied the man. "He's a dog, a Doberman, who stands upright, speaks, and carries a weapon. He is leading an army of mutant animals that is taking over Kennel in a most bizarre way. His weapon somehow makes dogs smart. Very smart. As smart as people. After he shoots the dogs with his weapon, they can talk and they can think. Right now they are in the process of taking over the whole planet."

The man picked up the collar that had been around his neck. "The dogs are then putting these enslavement collars on their human masters and forcing us to obey them. Sit up, roll over — well, you get the idea."

"How did you escape?" asked the emperor.

"My hobby happens to be fixing up old space-ships," answered the man. "I was working on this one-man craft when my dog, Buttons, stood on his hind legs, called me a few nasty names, then slapped this collar around my neck. It took every ounce of willpower I had, but I managed to climb into the ship and take off. I set the autopilot for your planet and hoped for the best."

"Wow!" exclaimed the emperor. "Great story! I mean, Doctor, get this man to the hospital. Examine him, make sure he's all right."

As the doctor led the man from Kennel to the nearest hospital, Emperor Jon raced back to his throne room. "A talking Doberman piloting a battle cruiser full of mutant animals?" he muttered to himself. "This could only be the work of Vetvix. This is very bad. It means that evil veterinarian has crawled back out from under the rock where she's been hiding. It also means that I've got to summon Pet Force!"

27

5

Back in his throne room, Emperor Jon pulled out a small computerized cauldron. The first few times that the emperor had needed to summon Garfield and his friends from their universe through the dimensional portal, he had called on his advisor, Sorcerer Binky. Binky would then use his cauldron to magically transport the five pets to Emperor Jon's universe. But Binky recently had given Jon his own computerized cauldron, tuned to the magical frequency that would pull the pets through the portal.

"Let's see," said Jon, staring at the remote control for the cauldron. "I believe it's this switch." He flipped a control and the thick brown liquid in the cauldron began to bubble furiously. "Nope," said Jon. "That's the button for quick-boiling soup. I'll use that later for lunch."

Jon concentrated, then pressed a few buttons. The bubbling stopped, the fluid in the cauldron became clear, and on the surface of the now-calm liquid an image appeared. It was the image of a backyard in our universe.

Our universe, Jon's backyard . . .

"Okay," said Jon as he stood beside the net that stretched across the backyard. "Here are the sides. It'll be me, Nermal, and Pooky against Arlene, Odie, and Garfield."

"In other words," began Arlene, "each side will have one inanimate team member. They've got Pooky, a stuffed teddy bear, and we've got Garfield, a stuffed orange blimp."

"Very funny, Arlene," said Garfield, who was now extremely cranky. "But you'll remember that this dumb game wasn't my idea. What's the point of hitting a stupid ball from one side of a net to the other if the object of the game is just to hit it back to the side it started on? Why not just leave it there and save us all a lot of trouble, not to mention" — Garfield braced himself to say the word he hated to mention — "exercise! Yuck!"

"You're just jealous because our side has better players," taunted Nermal.

"Oh, yeah," replied Garfield. "You, the teddy bear, and the geekasaurus. Quite a team. I'm sure the Chicago Bulls are quaking in their sneakers!"

"Okay, look alive!" shouted Jon. "Even you, Garfield!" Then he snickered at his little joke and served the ball.

The ball drifted over the net. "I've got it!" called Arlene. She took two steps to her right, then slapped the ball back over to Jon's side of the net.

"Mine!" shouted Nermal, sending the ball flying back with a two-handed shot. The ball headed toward Garfield.

"Take it!" Arlene called to Garfield, who was curled up in a classic loaf position. The fat cat looked up at the ball arching its way toward him. He yawned, then lazily stretched out a paw in the general direction of the ball, which was rushing back to earth. It landed inches from his furry mitt.

"Garfield!" shrieked Jon, Nermal, and, loudest of all, Arlene.

"You've got to make some effort," lectured Arlene. "It's the least you can do."

"That's what I'm best at," replied Garfield. "Doing the least I can do." Odie trotted over and drooled on Garfield's head. "If that's a plan to get me to move, it's not going to work. You see, moving is much too much like . . . exercise. There, I said it again. I'm exhausted. When's lunch?"

"Point for our side," yelled Nermal, very glad that Garfield was not on his team.

Jon served again. This time the ball headed right for Odie. *Oh, this is perfect*, thought Garfield. *That dumb dog wouldn't know what to do with the ball if it hit him right in the head!*

And, as a matter of fact, that's exactly what happened. The ball sailed right at Odie's head. He

POMP!

leaped up to meet it and slammed it back over the net with his thick canine skull. The ball went flying past Jon and Nermal. "I've got it!" called Jon, who turned his back to the net and started running at top speed, racing to try to get to the volleyball.

At that precise moment, Garfield, Odie, Nermal, Arlene, and Pooky disappeared.

The parallel universe . . .

Before the five pets realized what had happened, they found themselves standing in Emperor Jon's throne room. They had transformed into their Pet Force identities — Garzooka, Odious, Abnermal, Starlena, and Compooky. The superheroes stood before Emperor Jon.

Before anyone could say a word, Odious — who was thrilled to see the emperor again — trotted over and licked a slobbery greeting right on his face. Odious had, of course, forgotten about the effect of his super-stretchy stun tongue. He was simply being affectionate. The emperor passed out as soon as the powerful, wet tongue made contact with his face.

"We're back," said Garzooka. "And Odious is just as clever as always."

The others quickly rushed to the emperor's side and within a few minutes had revived him. "I do wish you would remember about your powers, Odious," the emperor said when he had regained his senses (at least the senses Emperor Jon had in the first place).

The others once again got used to their superhero bodies. Garzooka flexed his rippling muscles, Starlena hummed, warming up her hypnotic siren song, and sparkling shards of ice crackled from Abnermal's fingertips. Each time they appeared in Emperor Jon's universe, the five pets-turned-heroes grew more comfortable with their super bodies and powers. Except for Odious, of course.

"What is it that forces you to bring us back to your universe, your highness?" asked Compooky, all business as usual.

Emperor Jon quickly updated Pet Force on Vetvix, K-Niner, and the events that had taken place on Kennel.

"I knew we hadn't heard the last of Vetvix," said Starlena when Jon was finished with his story. "She was just in hiding, plotting her next vicious attack. We must go to Kennel and stop K-Niner."

Garzooka turned pale. "Intelligent, talking dogs running a planet?" he gasped. "I have to sit down." The stunned Pet Force leader took a seat and continued. "Dogs in charge? I knew Vetvix was bad, but I had no idea that she could stoop to something like this. Her evil truly knows no bounds. Intelligent dogs! This is a perverse crime against nature of the highest order. K-Niner must be stopped!"

"Get a grip, Garzooka," groaned Starlena, rolling her eyes. "We all get the message."

"Garzooka is right," put in Emperor Jon. "If K-Niner is not stopped, the entire universe will be dominated by dogs."

"I think I'm going to faint," cried Garzooka as he led Pet Force to their starship, the *Lightspeed Lasagna*. Emperor Jon always kept the ship ready and waiting in the palace garage. The five heroes boarded their vessel and took off for the planet Kennel. Emperor Jon monitored Pet Force from the communications center in his throne room. He watched as the *Lightspeed Lasagna* cleared the planet Polyester's atmosphere, and breathed a sigh of relief knowing that help was on its way.

6

On the other side of the universe, a small, makeshift spaceship called the *Planetary Pizza* drifted in a high orbit around the planet Glacia. Glacia was many light-years from the planet Polyester. It was the planet farthest from the sun in its solar system. Therefore, Glacia was one of the coldest, snowiest places in all of Emperor Jon's universe.

Inside the *Planetary Pizza*, Space Pie-Rat adjusted some knobs and switches on the ship's control panel. The panel was really an old car dashboard. Sorcerer Binky had pieced the ship together from secondhand parts. The sorcerer had built the ship for Pet Force because Pie-Rat had stolen their *Lightspeed Lasagna*. Later, Pet Force reclaimed the *Lightspeed Lasagna*, but then Pie-Rat escaped in the *Planetary Pizza* with the shattered pieces of Vetvix's power crystal.

Pie-Rat had come to Glacia to get Vetvix's broken crystal repaired. *At last*, thought Pie-Rat as he eased the ship into a lower orbit. *After searching half the universe, I have finally located Barfo the Evil Wizard — the one man who can help me restore the crystal.*

Pie-Rat peered out the cockpit window at the snowcapped mountains below. *I have to say that if I were an all-powerful wizard — a master of dark magic and all that — this giant ice cube would be the last place I would pick to call home, sweet home*, Pie-Rat thought. *But from what I hear, this guy likes his privacy.*

Pie-Rat guided the *Planetary Pizza* to a soft landing on a flat, open ice field near the base of a huge mountain. According to the ship's sensors, it was the highest mountain on Glacia. *I paid big bucks to my informant on the planet Data to find out the location of Barfo's planet*, thought Pie-Rat as he stepped from the ship. He strapped on his backpack, parka, and snow boots. *I'd hate to have come all this way for nothing. Still, if I find him and he can repair the crystal, unlimited evil power will be mine!*

Pie-Rat began the long, difficult climb up the mountain. According to the information he had bought, Barfo lived in a cave at the top of the mountain.

Up he went, through craggy passes and along slippery slopes. The higher he got, the colder and snowier the weather became. The wind bit his face

and the snow blinded him, but Pie-Rat still kept climbing.

The man he sought — Barfo — was actually the evil wizard who had trained Vetvix in black magic and helped her gain her dark powers. He was also the creator of the power crystal. After making the evil gem, he had given it to Vetvix, who was his favorite student. Pie-Rat assumed that the wizard who made the crystal would also be able to repair it. He had gambled a lot on this quest, but the reward, if he was successful, would be power beyond his wildest imagination.

Pie-Rat looked up, squinting, and was hit with a faceful of falling snow. He was colder than he had ever been in his whole life. Brushing the mound of white stuff off his face, he thought he saw the top of the mountain. Encouraged by this sight, he struggled onward until he reached the mouth of a cave near the mountaintop. He ducked inside. It felt good to be out of the wind and snow. Pie-Rat

pulled a candle from his backpack, lit it, and pro-
ceeded into the dark, winding cave. The air got
warmer and warmer as he went deeper into the
cave.

Suddenly someone stepped out right into Pie-
Rat's path. The startled rodent dropped his candle
and the cave went dark.

"Who's there?" called a rough but high-pitched
voice.

"I am Space Pie-Rat, and I seek Barfo the Evil
Wizard," replied Pie-Rat, trying desperately to
make out the figure that stood before him in the
dark. "I hold a power crystal that Barfo made
once, long ago."

"Go away!" came the answer. "Barfo sees no vis-
itors. I take care of that."

"But I bring a power crystal he made long ago,"
Pie-Rat repeated. He was worried that his journey had been for nothing. "I need his help to rejoin
its shattered pieces."

A flickering light filled the cave as the creature
before Pie-Rat relit the candle. Pie-Rat looked
down and saw a short, gnarled gnome holding the
candle. The gnome's skin was dried out and
cracked. His matted hair hung like dirty rags
down to his shoulders. The small, grotesque creature wore an old robe tied at the waist with a
length of rope. He now motioned for Pie-Rat to
follow.

"The crystal, eh?" cackled the gnome in his thin,

raspy voice. "Why didn't you say so?"

"I did say so," replied Pie-Rat.

"So you did," said the gnome. "Wise guy," he muttered under his breath. "Follow me."

"Who are you?" asked Pie-Rat as he followed the strange little man.

"I am Hobart the Gnome," replied the creature. "For three centuries I have been Barfo's faithful assistant. I keep away the riffraff — you know, insurance salesmen, planetary scouts selling magazine subscriptions and cookies, and the like. But since you possess the crystal, I will take you to Barfo."

Using only the candlelight as a guide, Hobart led Pie-Rat through a series of winding narrow tunnels. After what seemed to Pie-Rat like a long hike, the cramped tunnels opened into a huge cavern. The cavern was lit by two rows of burning torches, their light casting soft shadows on the cave walls. At the far end of the cavern, perched on a large throne made out of bones and skulls, sat Barfo the Evil Wizard.

Barfo was more than five hundred years old, but he didn't look a day over three hundred. His long white beard hung down to his sandal-clad feet. His flowing white hair extended from beneath a tall, pointy hat and draped over his slightly hunched shoulders. Barfo's wrinkled face reflected his centuries of experience. His eyes were a bit crossed, giving him a slightly confused look.

"Who is this stranger you bring before me, Hobworth?" asked Barfo.

"The name is Hobart, Master," replied the gnome. "You know, your faithful assistant for the past three hundred years?"

"Yes, yes, Hogarth," continued the wizard. "I know who *you* are. Who is this?"

"My name is —" began Pie-Rat.

"He was talking to me!" interrupted Hobart. "His name, Master, is Pie-Rat."

"I see," said Barfo. "Well, Tie-Back, what business do you have with — with . . . ?"

"Barfo the Evil Wizard," finished Hobart.

"I know my own name, Hodad!" snarled the wizard. "Young people, always in a hurry. Never let you finish a sentence."

"I was sent to you by my good friend Vetvix," explained Pie-Rat. "She gave me her power crystal as a token of our friendship. Unfortunately, the crystal shattered accidentally. I was hoping you could repair it."

"Ah, yes, Vetvix," mused the wizard. "My finest student. I remember her well. She was — whom was I talking about?"

"Vetvix, Barfo," replied the gnome.

"Vetvix-Barfo? Never heard of him," continued the wizard.

"The crystal, your wizardness," reminded Pie-Rat, trying to get the wizard back on track.

"The crystal?" replied Barfo. "I gave the crystal to Vetvix years ago. Haven't seen it since."

Pie-Rat reached into his backpack and pulled out a small sack that contained the shattered pieces of the power crystal. He emptied the contents of the sack into his outstretched hand. The glittering fragments of clear stone sat in a sparkling heap on his palm.

"The crystal," whispered Barfo, awestruck to be in its presence once again.

"Can you restore it?" asked Pie-Rat.

"Of course," replied the wizard. Barfo pulled out a dusty old book of spells and began to flip through its pages. "Let's see," he mumbled, reading the various entries in the book. "Carburetor repair, chocolate eclair filling, comic book pricing — ah, here it is. Crystal restoration."

The gnome scurried to the far side of the cave and quickly returned with a long, hinged, leather carrying case. He blew the dust off, then flipped open the cover. Inside was Barfo's magic wand. "Here you are, Master. Your wand."

As the torchlight flickered and the gnome sang a mournful chant, Barfo waved his wand in the air and recited an ancient spell:

"Oom-ba, doom-ba, silk and leather,
Make these pieces come together.
Oom-ba, doom-ba, sword and pistol,
Restore the magic to this crystal!"

The tip of Barfo's wand began to glow bright red. A magical energy field flew from the wand and surrounded the pieces of the shattered crystal, lifting them from Pie-Rat's hand. The fragments swirled in the air, held up by the red glow. They spun faster and faster, until finally the crystal was whole once again. The re-formed crystal floated over to Barfo and gently landed in his hand.

"Amazing!" exclaimed Pie-Rat, barely able to hide his excitement. "Wonderful! Thank you, O great wizard! Thank you!"

Pie-Rat then turned to thank Hobart for his help, but something strange was happening to the tiny gnome. His body began to twist and morph, losing its shape and growing in size. Caught in a mystical cyclone, his skin mutated and stretched. When the transformation was complete, the gnome had turned into Vetvix!

"Barfo, thank you for restoring my crystal," cackled Vetvix as Barfo handed her the magnificent gemstone. "And Pie-Rat, my old friend and new enemy, thank *you* for stepping right into my trap."

Pie-Rat turned pale, his moment of triumph instantly changed into disaster. "B-but how? How did you find me?" he stammered.

"My cosmic connection with the crystal allowed me to learn that it had been shattered," explained Vetvix. "I knew that you would do anything, go anywhere, to find a way to make it whole again. I figured that sooner or later your travels would bring you here.

"I arrived several days ago," Vetvix continued. "I hadn't visited with my old master for many years, so I took the chance to catch up. I cast a spell to give myself the gnome appearance, then waited for you to show up. Naturally Barfo's loyalties were with me, his finest student, so he agreed to be part of the plan. Isn't that right, Barfo?"

"Absolutely," replied the wizard. "I'd be happy to be part of your plan.

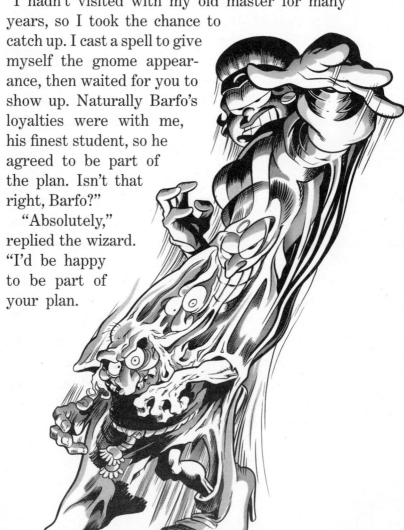

or two."

"Um, right," said Vetvix, rolling her eyes. "But now to the business at hand. I've been waiting a long time for this, Pie-Rat. Good-bye, old friend!"

Vetvix held the power crystal high above her head. She closed her eyes and focused her evil energy on the sparkling gem. A blinding light shot from the stone and surrounded Pie-Rat, who disappeared in a flash. He was instantly transported to the center of an asteroid hundreds of light-years away, trapped inside several miles of solid rock.

"Thank you, my master," said Vetvix as she prepared to leave. "I can now go on to the more important business of taking over the universe from Emperor Jon."

"Don't be such a stranger," said Barfo.

"I won't be," replied Vetvix, smiling.

"And don't you worry," continued Barfo. "When that Pie-Rat shows up, we'll be ready for him."

Vetvix rolled her eyes again at her master's absentmindedness. Then, using the power of her newly restored crystal, she disappeared in a flash of bright red light.

7

Meanwhile, aboard the *Lightspeed Lasagna*, Pet Force approached the planet Kennel.

"Sensors indicate a large battle cruiser still present on the planet's surface," reported Compooky.

"That means K-Niner is still down there," said Starlena.

Garzooka's face turned pale at the thought of a dog-dominated world. "Thinking, talking dogs? Ick!" he said, shuddering.

"Oh, I don't know," said Abnermal. "Dogs aren't so bad."

At that moment Odious came trotting by with a metal container stuck over his head. The container had held dog biscuits. When the Marvelously Muscled Mutt had tried to get at the biscuits, he caught his head in the container. He now stumbled around the ship blindly, banging into walls.

Garzooka stood up and yanked the container off, practically taking Odious's head along with it. "You were saying?" he muttered to Abnermal.

"Entering Kennel's atmosphere," announced Compooky.

"Here we go," said Garzooka. "Moving in for a landing."

Suddenly a laser blast from the planet's surface rocked the *Lightspeed Lasagna*. The ship spun out of control.

"That blast came from K-Niner's battle cruiser," reported Compooky. "I'm attempting to regain control of our ship."

Another round of pinpoint lasers struck the *Lightspeed Lasagna*, exploding in bright red bursts. Inside, the crew was tossed around the tiny cockpit like rag dolls.

"Abnermal!" shouted Garzooka, getting to his feet. "See if you can extend your force field around the ship."

"Good idea," replied Abnermal. He closed his eyes and concentrated deeply, extending his invisible force field around the *Lightspeed Lasagna*.

Laser fire again streaked from K-Niner's battle cruiser. The blast hit Abnermal's force field and deflected away. K-Niner fired again.

"My force field!" yelled Abnermal. "It's starting to weaken. I don't know if I can stop another hit!" The strain of protecting the entire ship was showing on his face.

The next shot from K-Niner's ship struck Abnermal's force field. Inside the *Lightspeed Lasagna*, Abnermal collapsed from exhaustion. "I'm sorry," he said, out of breath. "I couldn't hold on any longer."

One more blast from the battle cruiser made the unprotected *Lightspeed Lasagna* shudder. The ship burst into flames and plunged toward the planet below.

"We're going down!" shouted Starlena.

Garzooka rushed to a supply cabinet on the far side of the cockpit. "Here!" he said, pulling out parachutes and tossing one to each member of Pet Force. "Strap these on. We'll have to bail out once we've entered the planet's atmosphere. It's our only chance."

The five heroes put on their parachutes and waited by the *Lightspeed Lasagna*'s escape hatch.

"We've got to time this just perfectly," explained Compooky. "If we jump too soon, we'll burn up in the upper atmosphere. If we jump too late, the parachutes won't slow us down enough, and we'll hit the ground too fast."

"*You're* the hyper-intelligent supercomputer," said Abnermal. "*You* say when."

Compooky's brain worked at near light speed, calculating the rate at which they were falling, the distance to the ground, and the size of their parachutes. When just the right second arrived, he shouted, "*Jump!*"

Compooky popped the escape hatch, and Pet Force leaped from the burning spaceship. They plummeted toward the ground. Then, after a count of ten, they pulled their rip cords.

Compooky's parachute opened, blossoming in the sky like a red-and-orange flower. Starlena's opened next, then Garzooka's. Odious's chute had an automatic release, since the team wasn't sure he had the brainpower to pull the rip cord by himself. His parachute opened as well.

But Abnermal's parachute did not open.

The parachutes slowed the fall of the other Pet Force members, but Abnermal continued to drop, shooting past his friends. He acted quickly. Using his freeze-power, he shot a long icicle back up toward Garzooka, who knew exactly what to do. Garzooka reached out and grabbed one end of the icicle. Abnermal took hold of the other end and gripped with all his might. Slowly he climbed up the icicle, his hands slipping every inch of the way. Finally he reached Garzooka and wrapped his arms around his friend's waist.

The two heroes now shared one parachute.

"We're falling too quickly!" Garzooka shouted in order to be heard over the wind rushing past their ears. "With the extra weight, we're going to hit the ground too fast!"

"I told you not to scarf down every frozen pizza on the ship when we left on this mission!" Abnermal yelled back. "I don't suppose there's enough time for you to go on a crash diet before we make our crash landing!"

For once Garzooka remained silent. He stared

at the planet's surface, which was approaching them at frightening speed.

Then Abnermal came up with a plan. "I have an idea!" he shouted.

"This is a pretty good time for your first one ever," replied Garzooka.

Abnermal used his freeze-power to chill the moisture in the air around them. It began to snow. A blizzard of thick, white snowflakes drifted to the ground beneath them. When the two heroes finally touched down, they landed in a mountain of soft snow.

A short distance away, the *Lightspeed Lasagna* crashed into a snowbank. The tall mountain of fresh snow softened the ship's impact, as well. Starlena and Compooky landed gently right next to Garzooka and Abnermal. Odious landed in the snow nearby and started at once to build a snowman.

But right after Pet Force landed, K-Niner and his army appeared on the scene. The deadly, deranged Doberman lashed out with a powerful punch that sent Odious crashing into the snowman he had just finished. Then K-Niner leaped onto Abnermal's back and slammed him to the ground before the superhero could put up his protective force field.

A swarm of mutant soldiers attacked Garzooka and Starlena. The Pet Force leader fired gamma-radiated hairballs, but for each soldier he took out, two more appeared to continue the battle. Starlena sang out with her hypnotic siren song, but the troops were prepared. They popped in heavy-duty earplugs, which were strong enough to block the stunning effects of her magical melody. A few mutant soldiers who didn't get their earplugs in quickly enough collapsed, but the rest of the troops were protected from her siren song.

"Rousing good show, I say," barked K-Niner as he opened his massive jaws and prepared to sink his fangs into Abnermal's throat. "But now I'm afraid it's time for the curtain to come down on Pet Force. Permanently."

Abnermal acted swiftly. He blew a blast of freeze-breath into K-Niner's wide-open mouth. The frozen air shot down his throat, and the Doberman reeled back in shock, his paws clutching his neck.

"What's the matter, K-Niner?" said Abnermal. "Do I have bad breath?" Then he fired a freeze-blast at the super villain, encasing him in a solid block of ice. "I'd say 'That ought to put you on ice for a while,' but I always leave the bad jokes to Garzooka."

Abnermal jumped to his feet and joined Garzooka and Odious in the fight. Within a few minutes, Pet Force was winning the battle.

"Stop where you are or the teddy bear dies!" said a voice from behind them.

The other Pet Force teammates looked around

in a panic for Compooky. Compooky was in the talons of K-Niner's henchman, Wilbur the turtle-crow. Wilbur had a laser weapon pointed at Compooky's head. Normally the half-teddy bear, half-computer stayed behind with the *Lightspeed Lasagna*. He was more valuable to the team for his brains than his fighting ability. But this time, since they all had to escape the burning ship, Compooky had had no choice but to join the others. Now he was being carried off — a hostage of K-Niner's mutant army.

Garzooka, Starlena, Odious, and Abnermal stood helplessly. They could not do anything that would put Compooky in danger.

At that moment, K-Niner flexed his mighty muscles and broke free of the ice block. He snuck up behind the four Pet Force members and clubbed each one unconscious with his massive Doberman paw.

"Take them away," ordered K-Niner. "And bring me a cup of hot tea. I'm still shivering from that ice cube overcoat that annoying kitten trapped me in."

K-Niner's soldiers dragged off the four Pet Force teammates and threw them into a prison cell.

"Our task here is now complete," K-Niner announced to his troops. "It is time to move on to the next phase of our plan. Of course, with humans enslaved and dogs running this planet, Pet Force will just rot in a cell. But who ever said life was fair — even for superheroes? Ta-ta!"

K-Niner and his army returned to their battle cruiser and departed the planet Kennel, leaving Garzooka, Starlena, Odious, and Abnermal trapped in their jail cell. The Despicable Doberman of Doom also left behind a team of brain-boosted guard dogs who held Compooky hostage, ensuring that Pet Force would never leave the planet Kennel.

8

"Just exactly how will we get out of this one?" asked Abnermal when he and the others regained consciousness. He fired a freeze-blast at the thick steel bars of the cell door. A thin coating of ice covered the door, then quickly melted. "A freeze-proof cell. I should have known."

"Here, let me try," said Garzooka. "Odious, give me a hand." Odious jumped up and began to applaud, nodding and slobbering as if Garzooka had just finished performing a hit song.

"I meant help me with the door." Garzooka pointed at the reinforced steel door that kept them captive. "I think together we can rip this sucker right off its hinges." Garzooka and Odious each got a firm grip on the door. "On three," said Garzooka. "One, two —"

"Let go of the door or the teddy bear is history!" shouted one of the armed guard dogs that K-Niner had left in charge.

Garzooka peered out of the cell, and he saw five

canine guards holding huge laser weapons. He held tightly to the door. He didn't budge.

"Go tell the others to blast that brainy teddy bear into a million fuzzy pieces," ordered the guard who had shouted the first order. Several other guards started to move away.

Garzooka had no choice. The guard had called his bluff. "No! Wait!" he shouted, releasing his grip on the door. "You win. Just don't hurt Compooky."

"What about the mutt?" asked the guard, seeing that Odious still held tightly to the cell door, clueless about the threat to Compooky's life.

"Odious, let go of the door!" ordered Garzooka.

Odious didn't budge. Once again he was clueless. Garzooka turned to Abnermal. "Some help here, Abnermal?" he asked.

"Come on, Odious, let go of the door!" coaxed Abnermal.

"I meant a little help from your freeze-power," said Garzooka impatiently.

"Well, why didn't you say so?" shot back Abnermal, his super-feline pester-power really getting under Garzooka's skin. "You know, sometimes you can be —"

"*Just do it!*" screamed Garzooka.

"Okay! Okay!" whined Abnermal. "What a grouch!" Abnermal fired a freeze-blast at the door again. A thin layer of slick ice coated the door. Odious lost his grip and slipped off with a thud.

"My siren song should take care of those guards, Garzooka," said Starlena. "That'll give you another shot at ripping open the door." Odious and Abermal plugged their ears. (Garzooka was immune to Starlena's siren song.) Then Starlena stepped to the door and unleashed a powerful burst of singing that echoed throughout the prison hallways.

The guards went about their patrolling as if nothing had happened. "Heavy-duty earplugs again!" snarled Starlena, upset that her song had no effect. She turned to Garzooka. "I can't use my siren song, Abnermal can't use his freeze-power, and you can't bust us out of here or the guards will hurt Compooky, *wherever* he is! I hate to admit it, but Pet Force is paralyzed!"

The hours dragged on. Day slipped into night, and Pet Force grew more and more frustrated. They began pacing back and forth across the tiny square cell. "Watch where you're pacing, you big, muscle-bound oaf!" Abnermal snapped at Garzooka.

"*I'm* pacing here, you pestering little squirt," responded the Pet Force leader.

"Boys," said Starlena. "This is getting us nowhere."

Garzooka and Abnermal paused for a second and stared at each other, then continued to pace. Odious joined the pacing pattern, crisscrossing the cell and leaving a trail of drool behind him.

Suddenly all the lights in the prison went out. Pet Force stopped pacing and stood in the total darkness.

The entire prison was plunged into panic. Pet Force could hear the sound of the guard dogs yelling and stumbling over each other in the dark. Garzooka spat a gamma-radiated hairball into his hand. He held the glowing hairball up to the opening in the cell door and looked out. The hairball gave off enough light to reveal the confusion taking place in the hallway outside their cell. The guard dogs couldn't see anything in the darkness. They pulled out their earplugs so at least they would be able to hear as they tried to figure out what was going on.

"Here's our chance," said Garzooka, signaling to Starlena. Odious and Abnermal covered their ears. Starlena sang out, full voiced, with a hypnotic tune that immediately stunned all the guards within earshot. Garzooka grabbed the steel door to the cell and ripped it off its hinges. "Come on," shouted the Pet Force leader. "We are out of here!"

The four heroes rushed from their cell, led by the faint glow of Garzooka's radiating hairball. They stepped over the bodies of the stunned guard dogs as they made their way to the front door of the prison. Pet Force stepped outside. And ran right into Compooky!

"Compooky!" they all shouted at once.

"Are you all right?" asked Starlena.

"How did you escape?" asked Abnermal.

"Has K-Niner left the planet yet?" asked Garzooka.

Odious gave the hyper-intelligent part-computer, part-teddy bear a big hug and a couple of quarts of slobber as his way of saying hello.

"I will answer all your questions as we move," replied Compooky. "I suggest that we get back to the *Lightspeed Lasagna* at once."

Garzooka agreed and Pet Force headed off at top speed toward their ship. Compooky had a small light attached to the top of his head, powered by his own internal generator. He lit the way for his teammates. Garzooka was happy to get rid of his gamma-radiated hairball, because it was starting to burn a hole in his palm.

Compooky answered their questions as they hurried along. "I am unhurt," he told them. "K-Niner did not believe that I had the ability to escape. He did not think it was necessary to put me in a high security cell like the rest of you. He threw me into the basement of a nearby building and locked me in using only an electronic lock on the basement door."

Suddenly a team of guard dogs stepped into their path. "You will come with us . . . *now*!" commanded one of the dogs. Starlena sang out with her siren song, but this group of guards still had their earplugs in. Pet Force dove out of the way as the dogs opened fire.

Abnermal threw up his force field to protect the heroes. Odious fired his super-stretchy stun tongue again and again, knocking down guard dogs like dominoes. Garzooka took out a few with his gamma-radiated hairballs, and Abnermal hurled a freeze-blast that encased the remaining dogs in ice.

"Way to go, Pet Force!" exclaimed Starlena.

"It's nice to be back in action and back at full strength," added Garzooka.

Compooky continued with his story as they again raced toward the ship. "It didn't take me long to discover that the building K-Niner had locked me in contained the main power grid for the entire planet. I was able to access a computer and shut off all power on the planet from there. With the power off, the basement door popped open and I escaped. I also thought that the darkness would help you make your escape."

"You thought right, pal," said Garzooka. "Nice work!"

When the five heroes reached the *Lightspeed Lasagna*, they were shocked to find a crowd of humans gathered around the damaged ship. "Are you the heroes who freed us?" asked one of the humans.

"We have heard the story of the superpowered pets who came to stop the evil dogs from running our planet," said another.

Garzooka stepped forward. "We are Pet Force," he announced proudly, flexing his muscles in several classic bodybuilder poses. He looked around for cameras. There were none. "And I am Garzooka, leader of the team and much more good-looking, intelligent, and powerful than the others."

Starlena rolled her eyes and shoved Garzooka aside. "I am Starlena," she said. "And we are very glad to see that you are free from the control of the dogs."

"It seems that when I shut off the power on Kennel, the enslavement collars that had been holding the humans also stopped working," Compooky remarked.

"That is true," explained one of the humans. "People all over the planet are freeing themselves from the horrible collars."

"Well," said Abnermal, rubbing his hands together, "it looks like our work here is done."

"Not quite," said an older man. "Before you go pinning any medals on yourself, there are still these talking dogs to deal with!"

Abnermal frowned.

"He's right," said Garzooka. "The brain-boosted

dogs are still stronger than the humans, even without the enslavement collars to help them."

"I have an idea," said Compooky. "And I believe you good citizens of Kennel can help us. A short way back you'll find a group of unconscious guard dogs. Gather up as many of their brain-boosting weapons as you can and bring them back here to us. I think I can reverse the circuits on the weapons. Then we can use the weapons to return the dogs to their normal brainpower." All eyes turned to Odious. He slobbered and smiled.

"You mean zero brainpower," said Garzooka.

"Well, at least what they had before," replied Compooky.

"Like I said, zero, zip, *none!*" repeated Garzooka.

While the humans went off on their mission to gather up the brain-boosting weapons, Pet Force began to repair their damaged ship. The five heroes worked quickly and soon the *Lightspeed Lasagna* was fully repaired. The humans returned with about a dozen brain-boosting weapons. As Garzooka prepared the ship for takeoff, Compooky began changing the weapons so they would have the reverse effect.

"Thank you!" called out the crowd of waving humans as the *Lightspeed Lasagna* lifted off. "Our hopes rest with you, Pet Force."

Within seconds, the ship cleared Kennel's atmosphere and settled into orbit around the planet.

After Compooky finished his adjustments on the reverse–brain-boosting weapons, Garzooka placed them in the *Lightspeed Lasagna*'s gun ports. He began to circle the planet, bombarding it with the reverse radiation. The dogs whose brains had been boosted were returned to normal. Because the weapons were still set for the exact brainpower of dogs, the humans were unaffected by the radiation, and quickly regained control of the planet.

The humans on Kennel radioed their thanks to Pet Force. The horror on Kennel was over and the balance of pet/human power restored. The humans, however, gained new respect for their pets. Having seen things from the dogs' point of view helped the humans to think of their pets as more like friends. The dogs realized how much their owners really did care for them, and they happily resumed their roles as beloved pets.

On board the *Lightspeed Lasagna*, Garzooka's face turned deadly serious. "Now it's time to get that Despicable Doberman of Doom," he snarled. "Full speed!" he ordered, and the *Lightspeed Lasagna* zoomed off in hot pursuit of K-Niner's battle cruiser.

9

On board his battle cruiser, K-Niner settled back into the soft cushions of his command chair. He demurely sipped his tea and stared out the huge viewing window at the front of the ship. The stars sparkled against the rich blackness of space.

"Our takeover of Kennel was a smashing success," K-Niner announced to his mutant crew. "I must contact Vetvix at once and tell her of our victory." K-Niner sent a communications signal to Vetvix's *Floating Fortress of Fear*. He received a recorded message.

"Hello," the message said. "You have reached the hideout of Vetvix, the evil veterinarian. I'm not here right now. I'm probably out taking over a planet, plotting some revenge, or battling a super-hero team like Pet Force. At the sound of the beep, leave me a message and I'll get back to you as soon as I return to my *Floating Fortress of Fear*. BEEEEEEP!"

"K-Niner here," he began. "Ring me back when you return so I can tell you of my success on Kennel. Ta-ta for now!" Then he called out to his crew. "How long until we arrive at the next planet to conquer?"

Wilbur, the half-turtle/half-crow, scurried over to the command chair. The odd creature had become K-Niner's first mate aboard the battle cruiser, since he was one of the few crew members besides K-Niner who could speak. Wilbur pulled out star charts, then called up maps and readouts on a portable computer.

"I'd say," began Wilbur, getting himself tangled up in the huge charts, "figuring the distance between neighboring stars and factoring in the ship's fuel capacity and speed capability, the angle of approach and gravitational pull of nearby planets . . . I'd say — I have no idea."

K-Niner rested his head in his hands and wearily rubbed his eyes. "Why do I even bother to ask?" he muttered to himself.

"Beats me," replied Wilbur.

Just then a communications signal on K-Niner's control panel flashed and beeped. "Ah, that should be Vetvix returning my call," said the Despicable Doberman of Doom. The image of Vetvix came into focus on the small monitor before him.

"I got your message, K-Niner," said the evil veterinarian. "I was wrapping up some unfinished business with that traitor Space Pie-Rat. Don't *you* ever double-cross me or you'll end up in the middle of an asteroid, too."

"Heavens," replied K-Niner, "I wouldn't think of it." K-Niner then told Vetvix of his success on Kennel. (They didn't know that Pet Force had already freed the planet.)

"Considering your good work," snarled Vetvix, "I'm going to change your plans. Proceed at once to Emperor Jon's home planet, Polyester. No more pussyfooting — or should I say *'doggiefooting'* around. Let's go for the big cheese, the whole enchilada, the brass ring, the whole ball of wax, all the marbles —"

"Yes," replied K-Niner, cutting her off. "I get the idea."

"Never interrupt me when I'm on a roll!" shouted Vetvix, green smoke pouring from her ears. "Now full speed to Polyester and claim the emperor's throne for me!"

The *Lightspeed Lasagna* raced after K-Niner's battle cruiser, but even with the Pet Force ship's incredible speed, they couldn't catch up to the Despicable Doberman of Doom. By the time Emperor Jon radioed Pet Force in the *Lightspeed Lasagna* for help, K-Niner had already begun his assault on Polyester.

Garzooka stared at the viewscreen in front of him and listened in horror as the emperor told him what was happening on his planet. "Already entire villages have been enslaved by brain-boosted dogs," explained Jon. "The dogs have placed enslavement collars on their former masters, and —"

Emperor Jon's voice was drowned out by the sound of an explosion.

"Emperor Jon, what is it?" asked Garzooka in a panic.

"Oh, dear," replied Jon. "The brain-boosted dogs have started their attack on my palace. Hurry, Pet Force. If K-Niner takes the palace, my throne will fall to Vetvix. I can't —"

Then Garzooka's monitor went blank.

"Emperor!" shouted the Pet Force leader. No reply came from his speaker.

"Compooky, go check the main engines," ordered Garzooka. "See if you can squeeze some more power out of this ship. We've got to get to Polyester!"

As soon as the *Lightspeed Lasagna* entered the planet Polyester's atmosphere, a squadron of one-person fighter ships appeared from out of nowhere. They swarmed around the Pet Force ship like mosquitoes at a summer barbecue. Brain-boosted dogs sat at the controls of each tiny ship, firing laser blasts at the *Lightspeed Lasagna*.

Explosions jolted the ship. "We've been hit!" shouted Starlena. The next explosion knocked her to the floor.

10

"Abnermal, we need your force field!" shouted Garzooka as Odious helped Starlena to her feet. "That will buy us a few minutes to regroup!"

"You've got it!" replied Abnermal, extending his protective force field around the ship.

Garzooka gripped the piloting controls tightly and sent the *Lightspeed Lasagna* into a nosedive. Two fighter ships that had been closing in on the Pet Force ship from opposite sides slammed into each other and disappeared in a fiery explosion.

"That's two," said Starlena, scanning the area for the other fighters. "Three ships closing in from below," she announced.

Laser blasts from the three ships bounced off Abnermal's force field. "I can't hold this shield up forever," said Abnermal as icy beads of sweat formed on his forehead, then fell and shattered on the floor.

"Time to take this battle to the next level," snarled Garzooka. "Compooky, set the weapons systems to fire in automatic sequence on my command."

"Standing by," replied Compooky.

"That's it!" cried Abnermal, collapsing to the floor. "Force field's gone!"

"Now!" ordered Garzooka.

Compooky switched on the automatic weapons system just as Garzooka spun the *Lightspeed Lasagna* around and around like a pinwheel in space. Laser blasts sprayed out in all directions from the ship, blanketing space with deadly shots of energy. The three one-dog fighter craft tried to swerve out of

the way, but there was no escape from the shower of energy bullets that came at the tiny ships from every direction. Within moments, the *Lightspeed Lasagna* was alone in the sky.

"Well, that wasn't so bad," said Garzooka as he eased the ship toward the planet's surface. Starlena was still shaken from her fall. Abnermal had nearly passed out from using all of his energy on the force field. Odious was dizzy from the spinning of the ship, and he now stumbled around the cockpit, banging into walls. "All right," admitted Garzooka. "Maybe it *was* so bad!"

"I believe it's worse than that," said Compooky. "The reverse–brain-boosting weapons we brought with us from Kennel were destroyed by the blasts that hit our ship. Without them, we won't be able to return the dog population on Polyester to normal."

"As usual," replied Garzooka, "we'll have to make it up as we go along."

The *Lightspeed Lasagna* landed on the planet Polyester a short distance from Emperor Jon's palace. Pet Force leaped from the ship and found the planet in total chaos. A squad of dog soldiers opened fire on the superheroes.

Abnermal tried to throw his force field up, but he was still too weak from protecting the ship. Five dogs fired at once and Abnermal was thrown back against the outside of the *Lightspeed Lasagna*. Starlena sang out her siren song, but once again the dogs had prepared themselves with heavy-duty earplugs.

Garzooka swung into action. "Special delivery for doggies who are too smart for their own good," he shouted, firing gamma-radiated hairballs at the dogs in the front line of attack. The glowing globs of goo struck the laser rifles, melting each one. The melted steel dripped onto the hands of the dogs, burning them. The dogs ran away yelping.

Garzooka plowed into the second line of soldiers, his razor-sharp right claw glinting in the afternoon sun. "You furry failures look like you could use a shave," quipped the Pet Force leader. "A very close shave!"

As Garzooka slashed and punched several guards, five other guard dogs leaped onto Odious's back. Their boosted brains were no match for Odious's muscles. He grabbed one dog in each hand and flung them high into the air. Furious fists pounded the others into the ground, then Odious turned his attention to helping his teammate. Garzooka sidestepped a charging guard dog, then booted him in the behind, sending the dog flying. Odious quickly took care of the remaining guards.

"Nice welcoming committee," said Garzooka, catching his breath when the battle was over. "I wish they had baked us a cake."

"Me, too," said Abnermal, now fully recovered. "A nice big chocolate cake with tons of nuts and cherries and cream and —"

"Enough!" shouted Garzooka.

"But I haven't even gotten to the frosting!" whined Abnermal, using his pester-power. "Thick double fudge with caramel swirls and —"

Garzooka clamped his hand over Abnermal's mouth. Abnermal tried to continue talking. Odious stood next to Abnermal, drooling on his feet from all the talk of chocolate cake.

"I think we'd better split up," said Garzooka. "Starlena, you take Odious and Compooky and find the main power source on Polyester. If you can shut that down, the humans will be freed from their enslavement collars and that should even up the sides a bit."

"Good idea," said Starlena.

"I'll take Abnermal," Garzooka continued, wincing at the thought. "We'll head for Emperor Jon's palace." Garzooka removed his hand from Abnermal's mouth.

"— chocolate chips with marshmallows," said Abnermal, finishing his earlier sentence.

"Good luck, Pet Force," said Garzooka. "And let the fur fly!"

"Hey!" said Abnermal. "'*Let the fur fly.*' That would make a great T-shirt!"

Garzooka picked up Abnermal, tucked him under his arm, and dashed off toward the emperor's palace.

11

Garzooka and Abnermal stormed into Emperor Jon's palace. Brain-boosted dog soldiers were battling the emperor's elite palace guards.

Laser blasts exploded everywhere. Ancient stone walls crumbled and priceless statues were destroyed. Soldiers from both sides fell. The dog soldiers tried to take over the palace while the human guards struggled bravely to defend their emperor's home.

The two Pet Force heroes joined the battle. "It's Pet Force!" yelled several of the palace guards gleefully.

Garzooka bowed slightly. "Always nice to be recognized," he said as he pounded several dog soldiers with his ferocious fists. "But please, no autographs right now. This fight looks a bit too even for my taste. Time to make this into a one-sided battle!" He continued to smash away.

Meanwhile, Abnermal was taking great delight in firing freeze-blasts from each hand. His blasts covered dog soldiers in sheets of ice, freezing them where they stood like statues at a winter carnival. "Next bowler, step up to the line, please!" Abnermal shouted.

Garzooka grabbed one of the dog soldiers, and, flexing his powerful arm, rolled the soldier toward the group of frozen dogs that Abnermal had created. The rolling dog knocked down the group of icy canines like a bowling ball. Frozen dogs scattered everywhere. Only one of the soldiers remained standing. "Oh, well, I guess you can't get a strike every time," said Garzooka. Then he fired a gamma-radiated hairball at the remaining frozen dog. It exploded in a fiery flash.

The tide of the battle had turned. "It looks like the palace guards have this situation under control," said Garzooka. "Abnermal, follow me!"

"Aww, why can't I lead for a change?" moaned Abnermal.

A harsh look from Garzooka provided all the answer he needed. "All right! All right!" cried Abnermal. "Just don't carry me again. It makes me feel like a piece of luggage!"

Garzooka and Abnermal dashed up the circular stone staircase in the center of the palace. Pausing outside the door to Emperor Jon's throne room, Garzooka drew a deep breath and shouted, "Let the fur fly!"

"You said that already," sighed Abnermal. "And I still think it would make a great T-shirt!" Then the two heroes burst into the throne room.

"Ah," said K-Niner, who was sitting on the emperor's throne. "Two-fifths of the team known as Pet Force. I've been expecting you ever since I found out you escaped from Kennel. But I'm being rude. Allow me to introduce my guards."

Garzooka and Abnermal quickly glanced around the room at the guard dogs who stood ready, their weapons aimed at the two heroes.

"And I believe you know the emperor," continued K-Niner, pointing to Emperor Jon. The emperor was now stretched out on the floor with an enslavement collar around his neck. "He's really a fast learner. Watch. Sit up!" In response to K-Niner's command, Emperor Jon moved into a sitting position, his tongue hanging from his mouth. "Beg!" ordered K-Niner. Emperor Jon raised his arms and waved his hands, arms bent at the elbows. "Roll over!" The emperor dropped to the ground and rolled over, looking up and smiling like an obedient dog. "Now, for your final trick, hand over your kingdom to me!"

"That's enough!" shouted Garzooka, horrified to see the emperor in this condition — even dumber than usual. As he reached out to grab the enslavement collar that held Jon hostage, K-Niner grabbed onto Garzooka's wrist with a viselike grip.

"I've so enjoyed meeting you, Garzooka," said K-Niner as he tossed the Pet Force leader across the room. "Vetvix always said such nice things about you. It's almost a shame I'm about to destroy you."

"Don't get all mushy on me, K-Niner," replied Garzooka, picking himself up. He was stunned at just how powerful the Despicable Doberman of Doom was. "At least not until I pound you into a pile of canned dog food!"

"Garzooka, look out!" shouted Abnermal. An overanxious soldier aimed his weapon right at Garzooka's head. As the soldier fired, Abnermal grabbed the barrel of the laser rifle and yanked it upward. The blast ripped out a section of the throne room's ceiling. The chunk of ceiling now plunged toward Garzooka.

Abnermal quickly extended his force field above Garzooka's head. The chunks of falling stone bounced off the energy field and Garzooka was unharmed. "Nobody messes with my buddy Garzooka!" shouted Abnermal as he fired freeze-blasts at the soldiers.

"Thanks, pal, I didn't know you cared," replied Garzooka. But suddenly K-Niner was back upon him.

"We're all frightfully clever," said K-Niner as he pinned Garzooka to the cold stone floor. "But talk is inexpensive. Show me what you're made of."

"Sugar and spice and about fifty pounds of lasagna," quipped Garzooka as he shook K-Niner off and sprang to his feet. "And — oh, yeah — solid muscle." Garzooka threw a mighty punch that sent K-Niner sailing through the air. The Doberman landed hard against the throne.

"Thank you for flying Pet Force airlines," said Garzooka as he rushed toward K-Niner. "Our captain apologizes for the rough landing. Now please leave your face in the upright position so I can pound it!"

Garzooka and K-Niner rolled around the floor. Garzooka's massive muscles struggled against K-Niner's mutant power.

Meanwhile, Abnermal fired freeze-blasts at K-Niner's troops. "Chill out, guys," he quipped. "Oops, I promised I'd leave the bad jokes to Garzooka."

One of K-Niner's soldiers dived to the floor to get out of the way of Abnermal's freeze-blast. The soldier's brain-boosting weapon accidentally fired, striking Emperor Jon.

Normally, brain-boosting weapons did not affect humans because they were programmed for dogs. However, it just so happened that Emperor Jon had exactly the same brainpower as a dog. As the brain-boosting ray washed over the emperor, the blank expression on his face changed to one of deep thought and high intelligence. Although his enslavement collar still kept him under K-Niner's control, preventing him from joining the battle, Jon now stood upright and spoke in a deep voice.

"The sum of the squares of the two sides of a right triangle that form the right angle is equal to the square of the hypotenuse," announced the emperor, reciting a famous mathematical formula.

"Looks like your little toy can do more than turn dopey dogs into vicious, murdering beasts," said Garzooka as he gained the upper hand on K-Niner.

"That's '*Mr.* Vicious, Murdering Beast' to you," snarled K-Niner, kicking Garzooka off with his powerful hind legs. "The weapons are set for the brainpower of dogs. That doesn't say much for your glorious emperor."

"I think, therefore I am," said the emperor, deep in thought about the meaning of this bit of philosophy.

"And I slash, therefore I am," said Garzooka, extending his razor-sharp right claw.

K-Niner clamped down on Garzooka's right wrist with his long, sharp Doberman teeth, and the two titans continued their evenly matched struggle.

"Really, gentlemen," said Emperor Jon, noticing the battle before him. "Violence never solved anything. It was the philosopher Thomas Hobbes who said 'The first law of Nature is to seek peace and follow it.' Naturally I agree!"

And so Jon continued to show off his newly boosted brain while Abnermal held the troops at bay and Garzooka battled K-Niner.

12

Meanwhile, the other members of Pet Force had located the planet's main power station. "I see two guard dogs outside the entrance," said Starlena, who had taken command of her team. "You can be sure there are more inside." Turning to Odious, she added, "Odious, if you can take out those two guards, that will at least get us inside."

Odious nodded, then trotted over to the two brain-boosted guard dogs.

"Well, what do you know?" said one of the guards. "Here's a dog we missed with our brain-boosting rays. Big fellow, too. Lots of muscle." The guard dog raised his weapon and aimed it right at Odious. "Come here, pal," he said. "I've got something for you."

Odious struck the first guard with his super-stretchy stun tongue. The brain-boosted dog collapsed in a total mental meltdown.

"Hey!" shouted the second guard. "What's up with that?"

Odious picked up the first guard and slammed him into the second. The two crumpled in a heap, no match for Odious's incredible strength.

"Nice work," said Starlena. "Now open that door." Odious ripped the steel door from its hinges and the three Pet Force teammates stepped inside the power station.

Alarms sounded and a squadron of guard dogs raced toward them.

"Cover your ears," Starlena shouted to Odious. Then she sang out, unleashing her powerful siren song. *"Ah-ooooooo!"* It had no effect. These guards had also been given heavy-duty earplugs.

"I have an idea," said Compooky, racing to a nearby computer terminal.

"Well, whatever you're going to do, do it fast!" shouted Starlena. "Those guards are almost on us!"

Compooky found the power station's communications system and spoke into a microphone. His voice boomed out over a loudspeaker system. "Attention all guards! This is K-Niner with new orders for you!"

The guard dogs stopped running. "Did you hear something?" one dog asked another.

"I think I heard K-Niner," said a second dog, "but I'm not sure because I'm wearing these earplugs."

"What?" asked a third dog. "I can't hear you. I have my earplugs in."

"This is K-Niner!" Compooky shouted over the speaker system again, even louder than the first time. "Anyone who does not follow my new orders to the letter will be executed at once!"

One by one the guard dogs removed their earplugs so they could hear the message they believed was coming from their boss. "Now, Starlena!" cried Compooky when the last guard had removed his earplugs.

"*Ah-ooooooo!*" sang Starlena. This time the guards fell into a deep, hypnotic trance. Luckily, Odious still had his ears covered.

As the three Pet Forcers made their way to the main power grid, Compooky examined a brain-boosting weapon that he had taken from a fallen guard. "I have a plan that might just put an end to this madness once and for all," he stated when they had reached the grid. "If I reverse this brain-boosting weapon and also reverse the electrical charge on the power grid, I believe I can create an overload that would spread electrical energy all over the planet. This energy would contain radiation that should reverse the brain-boosting effect on the dogs."

"Whatever," said Starlena. "Just do it fast. Those guards won't sleep all day!"

Compooky worked quickly with determination. As the first of the unconscious guards began to stir, Compooky was ready. He turned the levels on the power grid to full, then fired the reversed–brain-boosting weapon into the grid.

Wave after wave of electrical energy flowed through the power grid, surging out all over the planet. In the skies above Polyester, a huge electrical storm formed, covering the planet with lightning.

The lightning contained the reverse–brain-boosting radiation. As lightning struck all over the planet, the brain-boosted dogs returned to normal. But the lightning storm had another effect as well. The electrical surge zapped the enslavement collars that were on the humans. The collars stopped working, and the people of Polyester were once again free.

In the throne room of Emperor Jon's palace, K-Niner had Garzooka pinned down. "So this is where it ends for you, my good chap," snarled the Despicable Doberman of Doom, tightening his death grip on Garzooka's throat.

"You know," said Jon, still spouting words of wisdom from his boosted brain, "Albert Einstein once said, while discussing his theory of relativity —"

Suddenly a lightning flash filled the throne room, blinding everyone for an instant.

"— what a pretty palace," said Jon, finishing his sentence as he looked around. "It's a lucky guy who gets to live here. Hey! Wait a minute. I get to live here. I'm the emperor." Then he reached up to his throat. "What's this thing doing around my neck?" he asked, removing the collar. "It doesn't go with my outfit at all."

When Garzooka's vision cleared, he saw K-Niner — once again a normal dog — sniffing around the floor and whining like a puppy. All around the planet Polyester, dogs returned to normal, and their former human prisoners once again became the masters.

Starlena, Odious, and Compooky arrived at the throne room and explained what had happened. Emperor Jon was also filled in on the events that took place during the time his brain went on its roller-coaster ride from obedient pet to brain-boosted genius.

"Things appear to be under control here," said Garzooka. "It looks like our work is done."

"Thank you, Pet Force," said the emperor. "Once again you have saved my universe and my throne. Although I seem to have developed a terrible rash around my neck. I think tight collars are out for me. From now on, it'll be V-necks only."

Emperor Jon sighed. "I suppose you guys want to return to your own universe now." He pulled out the small computerized cauldron he had used to bring Pet Force from their universe to his. He adjusted the controls on the remote, and the murky liquid in the tiny cauldron began to bubble furiously. "Good-bye," said the emperor. "Thank you once again." Then a puff of brown smoke filled the room.

When the smoke cleared, Pet Force was still standing next to Emperor Jon!

"What happened?" asked Starlena.

"I don't know," replied Jon. "The setting is right. The liquid is at the correct temperature. You should have been transported back home."

"Allow me to take a look, your highness," suggested Compooky. The half-computer/half-teddy bear took the remote control from the emperor and studied the cauldron for a few minutes. "It appears that something is blocking us from passing through the dimensional portal."

"What does that mean in plain English?" asked Abnermal.

"It means," explained Compooky, "that we can't go home. We are trapped in this universe!"

"We've got to get back!" cried Garzooka. "Jon can't make it without us. He'll forget about the lasagna in the oven and burn the whole house down. Or maybe he'll get another cat and give him my supper dish! This is terrible. We must get back to our universe right now! But how?"

Epilogue

Our universe, Jon's backyard . . .

"**I**'ve got it!" called Jon Arbuckle. He turned his back to the volleyball net and started running at top speed, racing back to try to get to the ball that had just been hit to him off of Odie's head. Jon dashed toward a hedge of low bushes that formed the border of his backyard. Diving for the ball, he crashed into the hedge headfirst, his orange sneakers waving in the air. The ball sailed over the hedge into the neighbor's yard.

"I'm all right, guys," shouted Jon. "Don't worry." He slowly pulled himself from the bushes and turned back, expecting to see Garfield, Odie, Arlene, Nermal, and Pooky. But when Jon turned around, his pets were gone. They had vanished, seemingly into thin air.

"Huh?" said Jon, using one of his favorite expressions. "Hey, guys!" he called out. "Guys? Where did you go?" he wondered.

* * *

This was certainly not the first time that Garfield and the others had disappeared into the parallel universe to go on a Pet Force adventure. However, due to the difference in the way time moved in the two universes, Pet Force was able to live through lengthy adventures in the other universe while only seconds passed in ours. They had never been away long enough for Jon to miss them. But this time things were different. For the first time ever, Jon noticed that his five pets were gone.

Where in the world could they be? he wondered. The answer, of course, had nothing to do with the world as Jon knew it. . . .